Let's Connect!

Thank you so much for taking the time to read this story. It's one of many and I pray that it will bless and inspire you in some way! I would love to hear your positive feedback as well as your constructive criticism on this story so that I can continue to grow and develop in my skill as a writer and author! When you have time, please contact me and/or provide your feedback at one of the links below! God bless and thank you in advance for your love, continued prayers and support.

Sincerely,
Author Aundrya Schnel

www.authoraundryaschnel.weebly.com
www.facebook.com/writeronamission
*Instagram: @writer.on.a.mission

****PLEASE POST A REVIEW ON AMAZON!!****
YOUR REVIEWS MEAN EVERYTHING!!

I dedicate this story to the men and women (*young and old*) who have experienced any form of abuse or manipulation at the hands of a pastor or leadership in the church! Time out for calling this "*church hurt*" and making those victimized out to be the bad guy for the sake of "*covering their pastor*"! What we are witnessing today in the pulpits is not how the true church was ever established and until leadership repent and turn from their wicked, unbiblical and manipulative tactics, there will continue to be a great falling away from the faith...

God Bless,
Author Aundrya Schnel

"The church is the only place where you can get robbed and nobody calls the police!"
~LeAndria Johnson

"The person who didn't get picked for kickball, can become pastor..."
~Sharde Martin

Jeremiah 5:26-29 (MSG)
*"My people are infiltrated by wicked men,
unscrupulous men on the hunt. They set traps for the
unsuspecting. Their victims are innocent men and
women. Their houses are stuffed with ill-gotten gain,
like a hunter's bag full of birds. Pretentious and
powerful and rich, hugely obese, oil with rolls of fat.
Worse, they have no conscience. Right and wrong
mean nothing to them. They stand for nothing, stand
up for no one, throw orphans to the wolves, exploit the
poor. Do you think I'll stand by and do nothing about
this? God's decree. Do you think I'll take serious
measures against a people like this?"*

Jeremiah 6:13-15 (MSG)
*"Everyone's after the dishonest dollar, little people and
big people alike. Prophets and priests and everyone in
between twist words and doctor truth. My people are
broken--shattered and they put on Band-Aids, saying
"It's not so bad, you'll be just fine." But things are not
"just fine"! Do you suppose they are embarrassed by
this outrage? No, they have no shame. They don't even
know how to blush. There's no hope for them. They've
hit bottom and there's no getting up. As far as I'm
concerned, they're finished. God has spoken..."*

INTRODUCTION

"What are you doing here?"
"We need to talk to you. We were told you were in this area..."
"Okay, you found me. What's up?"
"We need to buy a gun..."
"Two guns!"
"Oh okay, Bonnie and Clyde! You and your little girlfriend here want guns to prove your love?"
"Man, this is my sister and yeah, we're both buying..."
"Are you going to sell it to us or what?"
"I usually wouldn't ask so many questions but I really don't know you..."
"Well, we're not cops or anything..."
"Who did you say sent you my way?"
"Our uncle told us. His name is Tone..."
"Tone as in Big Tone?"
"Yeah, that's him..."
"Tone has guns that I'm sure he can sell you or give you to use since you're family..."
"We didn't ask him all that, we just told him we needed to buy guns..."
"Why is he sending you to me? We're not friends..."
"He said the cops were watching him right now so he has to play it cool for a while..."
"The cops want Tone? Since when? They never mess with him..."

"Man, I don't know but that's what he told us. Look, we got some business to handle so can we get these guns and get out of here?"
"Who's the target?"
"Nobody you care about, trust me..."
"How do you know? Who is it?"
"Our uncle said you wouldn't know them so I'm not saying..."
"Alright, my guns aren't cheap. Are you sure you want to waste your money?
"It's not a waste for us and we can buy whatever you have..."
"Yeah, this revenge is worth every dollar..."
"Is it worth dying over?"
"Yeah, it is! But we're not going to die. They are..."

FOR MY PASTOR IX
To Die Four

Charisma Jordan has been attending the same church since she was eighteen and she's been in charge of the evangelism team for the last eleven years. Charisma is a single mother to her 24-year-old son, Chase and her three daughters; 23-year-old Charisma *(who goes by Ceejai)*, 21-year-old Channing, and 20-year-old Charity. Last year, Charisma started having problems with her health and four months ago she had to step down as the leader for evangelism after being put on bed rest by her doctor. Her pastor, Bishop Harold Marshall, III didn't hesitate to assist Charisma when he agreed to cover her medical expenses in addition to giving her extra money for her bills, food and other necessities. While a gesture such as this would usually be very generous, there was a reason that Harold agreed to do all of this for her from a secret bank account he has outside of the church that no one including his wife knows about. Harold is convinced his money will keep his many secrets buried but time will soon reveal everything and Charisma's loyalty to her pastor will be tested in a way she doesn't anticipate.

It's a typical Friday morning as Charisma sits at her dining room table inside of her five bedroom home in the suburbs of Atlanta reading the newspaper and drinking her coffee. As glamorous as it seemed with Charisma's large house, white Mercedes Benz and a black Lexus parked in the garage, there was pain behind it all. Pain that Charisma carried and passed down to her children which caused Charisma's relationship with them to be nonexistent. Charisma didn't want to face her problems and deal with her many demons so she tried buying what money could not pay for. Her children grew up with the best clothes, they went to the best schools and they didn't want for anything. But Charisma was soon able to see that what she bought her children never eased their pain nor did it make things better. Chase and Ceejai live in Atlanta but they hardly ever come to see their mom and they ignore her calls most of the time. Channing and Charity applied to schools outside of the state when they were in high school, determined to get as far away from Charisma as they could. They made good on their promise when they applied to the University of Central Florida in Orlando and were accepted with full ride scholarships. They visit Atlanta often to see Chase, Ceejai and other family but they never talk to their mother even though she writes and calls every day to talk to them.

As Charisma finished her coffee, she received a call from the security guard at the front gate who said that her half-sister, Janelle was asking to be let inside. Charisma paused a moment as the guard waited for her response. Charisma tries not to talk to Janelle if she doesn't have to because she feels like she's being judged and she feels that Janelle looks down on her because she's married and active in ministry with her husband and Charisma never married. Charisma walked back into the kitchen to pour herself a glass of wine and she told the guard to let Janelle inside as she walked outside to the back patio near the pool to sit down. Moments later as she heard Janelle's car outside in the driveway, she sent her a text message and told her to come around to the back patio door.

"So you weren't going to let me inside, were you Charisma?" Janelle asked as she walked in and sat across from Charisma who was continuing to drink her wine and look at her phone.

"I let you in didn't I?" she asked.

"Yeah after making the guard sit on the phone almost five minutes waiting for you to respond!" Janelle replied in a stern tone.

"Well, I said yes so we can move on. What are you wearing?" Charisma asked, finally making eye contact with Janelle.

"Just one of the shirts from our conference at church." Janelle replied.

"So you and Vincent are still serving under that kid who calls himself a pastor?" Charisma asked, laughing sarcastically.

"Charisma Elise, don't start with me! I've told you about disrespecting our pastor just because he's young! He's as qualified as any other leader out here, probably more!" Janelle said, defensively.

"Girl please, your pastor is not much older than Chase! He's not married and he doesn't even have a Bishop!" Charisma replied as Janelle sighed in frustration.

"I didn't drive out here to go back and forth with you about Pastor Williams. But I will tell you this, my pastor has one thing your so-called Bishop does not have!" Janelle said.

"Oh really Janelle? What's that?" Charisma asked.

"He has character and he's pure!" Janelle replied as Charisma started laughing again.

"Girl, please! Men will be men and as young as your pastor is, I know he has to be doing something with somebody to be in leadership without a wife." Charisma said.

"I know it's hard for you to believe but he's not doing that. My pastor has sanctified himself to honor God and to lead God's people the right way without tainting them and damaging their souls. Can you say that about your leader, Charisma?" Janelle asked.

"Listen, I'm done talking about this Janelle! Why did you drive all the way to my house?" Charisma asked.

"Well for one, why didn't you tell any of us that you had been sick and that you're now on bed rest?" Janelle asked as Charisma sighed and shook her head.

"I told my kids and they didn't say anything so I didn't say anything else about it. Bridgette knows but I told her not to talk to you guys about it but I guess she said something anyway." Charisma replied.

"I didn't know you told Bridgette and I can't believe she kept something like that from us." Janelle said.

"Well, I told her to do it so don't hassle her. If Bridgette didn't tell you, who told you?" Charisma asked.

"Chase mentioned it to me when we talked but he thought I already knew." Janelle replied.

"So he came to see you? What about my daughters?" Charisma asked.

"I've been talking to them too and they visit us as well." Janelle replied.

"So all these visits with my kids and you never told them to come see their mother?" Charisma asked.

"Look, I ask them if they've talked to you and it's the same answer every time. I try to encourage them to visit you but they're grown, I can't force them to come see you!" Janelle replied.

"You could stop seeing them until they do see me." Charisma replied as Janelle paused a moment before responding.

"Have you lost your mind? You think I'm going to stop talking to my nieces and my nephew for you? That will never happen! Don't you think it's about time you stop playing this game and putting on this front and face the facts?" Janelle asked as Charisma took another sip of her wine.

"What are you talking about?" Charisma asked.

"C'mon Charisma, stop playing with me! You know exactly what I'm talking about. You have walked around for as long as I can remember acting like you're a better Christian than me because you went to a large and popular church but I attend a small ministry with only a few people." Janelle said.

"You and Vincent chose to go to that small church. I told you the perks my Bishop was ready to offer you if you came to our church but you didn't want it so don't hate now because you see how blessed I am!" Charisma replied as Janelle laughed sarcastically.

"Girl, stop it! I know good and well you don't think for even a minute that I'm jealous of you! I could care less about your big house and fancy cars or your "perks" as you put it at your church. My husband and I were not about to sell our souls for some money and popularity! You did it and look what it got you, Charisma! You have all these material things, you lavished your children with material things and it did nothing for their soul!" Janelle said.

"That's not true, it did plenty!" Charisma replied.

"Wow! So you think because your kids went to college that fixes everything? You raised all four of your children in that church and none of them are saved and none of them want anything to do with the church." Janelle said, sternly.

"Well like you said Janelle, they're grown. I can't control what they do when they become adults." Charisma replied.

"The Bible says that if you train your kids up in the way they should go, they won't depart when they are older. So my question now is what kind of training were you giving them?" Janelle asked as Charisma shook her head.

"I know you're not trying to question how I've raised my kids when you and Vincent don't even have any!" Charisma said, defensively.

"You can throw me and Vincent choosing not to have kids in my face all you want but I know there's a reason behind this and I'm almost afraid to find out what it is because it will only make me feel more guilt." Janelle replied as Charisma's expression changed.

"Guilt about what, Janelle?" Charisma asked.

"Guilt for not going with my first instinct when the kids were young and having them live with us." Janelle said.

"What? You were going to take my kids from me?" Charisma asked.

"Yeah, we wanted to after all the rumors we kept hearing about the abuse. But we had no proof your kids were in danger and every time I asked the kids if anything was going on that they wanted to talk about, they said everything was fine." Janelle said.

"I can't believe my ears right now! You questioned my kids about being abused? You really think I would let that happen to them?" Charisma asked, disgusted.

"I know you will do anything to keep the perks and your status in the church and whether you choose to tell me the truth or not, I know something happened to your kids and it will only be a matter of time before it comes to light." Janelle said.

"Nothing happened to them, Janelle so stop fishing!" Charisma replied.

"Charisma, what's going on with your kids' father? I mean, do they have the same dad or what?" Janelle asked.

"I told you a long time ago I didn't know who their father was, why are you asking now?" Charisma asked.

"I think you know who their father is and for some odd reason, you've been covering it up which to me could only mean one thing." Janelle said.

"Oh, and what's that Janelle?" Charisma asked with a smirk as she continued to drink her wine.

"You more than likely got pregnant by someone at your church, a leader perhaps." Janelle replied as Charisma laughed sarcastically. "I'm not joking!"

"You sure about that? This conclusion you've drawn is funny to me and it's clear that you will do anything to make me look bad and convince yourself that you're better than me!" Charisma said.

"Charisma, I'm done trying to convince you that I've never looked down on you or thought I was better than anybody. Furthermore, I don't need to make you look bad because if this is true; it will all come out on it's own. God's judgement begins at His house, meaning His church! I know unholy things have gone at your church and I know that whatever took place has to do with why your kids feel the way they do!" Janelle replied in a stern tone.

"Oh wow Janelle, when did this feeling of yours hit?" Charisma asked.

"I've known for years something isn't right and now I'm done just sitting back praying, I want answers after the bombshell Chase dropped on us." Janelle replied.

"What bombshell Janelle? What are you talking about?" Charisma asked.

"Two months ago, my pastor told Vincent and I to prepare our house for two children who would end up staying with us. We really didn't know that was possible considering Vincent and I never tried to adopt but my pastor is a real prophet so we did what he said and on Monday; we got the surprise of our life." Janelle said as Charisma's expression changed.

"What surprise?" Charisma asked.

"Chase showed up to our house in tears and you know he never cries!" Janelle said.

"What? He was crying? What happened?" Charisma asked in a concerned tone as Janelle sighed and shook her head.

"Chase came to our house and he had these twin boys with him. He asked could we talk and I let them inside wondering what he was about to say. Charisma, Chase is a father and those boys he showed up with are his 4-year-old identical twin sons." Janelle replied as Charisma reacted to what she said.

"Chase has two 4-year-old twin boys and he didn't tell me about them? He told you but he wouldn't tell their grandmother?" Charisma asked, disgusted.

"No he didn't tell you which concerns me in more ways than one and it was what made me come see you today! Chase asked for Vincent and I to keep his sons so they would be safe and have the chance at a better life than what he had." Janelle told her.

"He said that? He didn't enjoy all the things I gave him?" Charisma asked.

"No Charisma, it seems that money can't buy everything and your money did not change the outcome of your own children's lives!" Janelle replied.

"Did you forget that Chase and Ceejai are college graduates and my other two daughters are in college right now?" Charisma asked.

"I haven't forgotten anything! I'm very proud of them but a piece of paper can't heal wounds and you should know that Charisma." Janelle said as Charisma sighed in frustration.

"Okay fine, so when can I see my grandsons?" Charisma asked as Janelle paused a moment before responding. "What is it?"

"I took a picture of the boys before I left to come here. Here they are, Chase, Jr. is on the right but we call him by his middle name, Domonick and Cameron is on the left." Janelle replied showing Charisma a picture of them on her cell phone.

"Oh my God, these are my grandsons? They are beautiful! Wow! So when I can see them?" Charisma asked anxiously as Janelle shook her head.

"Charisma, I showed you that picture because Chase made me and Vincent promise him something before he left the boys with us." Janelle said as Charisma's expression changed.

"Okay, what was it?" she asked.

"He made us promise that we wouldn't allow you to see his sons or spend any time with them, not even if we're around. He doesn't want them to have anything to do with you." Janelle said as Charisma tried to fight back tears.

"So you let my son tell you to keep my grandsons away from me?" Charisma asked in a stern tone.

"Yes, I did! They're his sons so it's his choice! I asked him if he was sure he wanted to take it that far and he said yes so we promised and I was nice enough to let you see a picture of them but that's it Charisma. You need to respect Chase's wishes." Janelle said.

"What if I don't? I know where you live, Janelle!" Charisma said.

"Yeah, I know that and so does Chase. Listen Charisma, don't make this difficult. Chase told us if you tried to visit the boys, he would have a restraining order put in place. Don't make him do that, please!" Janelle said.

"So that's it? I never get to see my grandsons?" Charisma asked.

"For now you can't but maybe if you respect your son's wishes and own up for whatever it was that has caused your own children to want nothing to do with you, that can change." Janelle said as tears fell from Charisma's face.

"Can I ask you something?" Charisma asked.

"Sure, what is it?" she asked.

"Where's Domonick and Cameron's mother? Do I know her?" Charisma asked.

"Oh yeah, I forgot to tell you about her. It was Chase's ex-girlfriend, Shanika. You know they dated on and off all through high school." Janelle said as Charisma nodded.

"Yeah, I remember Shanika. So she came with Chase when he dropped off the boys?" Charisma asked.

"No, Shanika was actually the one keeping the boys at her apartment. Chase would just come by to visit them and drop off money since Shanika didn't have him on child support. Shanika had a mental breakdown and she tried to kill herself while the boys were sleeping in the other room." Janelle said.

"Oh my God! She attempted suicide while the boys were inside the apartment with her? Did she survive?" Charisma asked in a panic.

"Yeah, she got lucky. Chase happened to find her when he came by to see his sons and she was barely breathing after taking two bottles of pills. It's only the grace of God that she's still alive. But she's in a mental health facility now and they placed the boys with Chase but Chase was honest enough to admit that he runs the streets from time to time when he's not at work and he didn't want that for his sons so he brought them to us. He still plans to give money to us for them just like he did when they were living with Shanika and we told him he can see his sons anytime. Vincent and I prayed for him before he left." Janelle replied.

"So is Chase letting you take his sons to your church?" Charisma asked.

"Yeah, he is. He knows I don't go to your church so he was okay with it. Charisma, what aren't you telling me? Something is clearly wrong after everything that just happened and in spite of what you think I feel about you, I love you Charisma! You're my big sister and I have always looked up to you. We used to be close and we used to talk about everything." Janelle said as she took Charisma by her hands.

"You still consider me your big sister?" Charisma asked.

"Girl yes, that won't ever change! I don't like everything you do and I'm always going to stand for the truth but it doesn't mean I love you any less. Charisma, I won't force you to talk to me but I am here if you change your mind and I hope you make the decision to come clean about whatever is going on before it's too late." Janelle replied as Charisma sighed and thought for a moment before responding.

"So what do you want from me?" Charisma asked.

"I want you to be honest and own your truth! You may walk around like you're so strong but you don't like the way things have turned out with you and your kids' relationship. But you're not going to repair anything putting on a front." Janelle replied.

"So you want me to tell you everything now?" Charisma asked.

"Charisma, it's not about you telling me everything. It's about being honest with yourself and having an honest conversation with your kids and making amends for whatever took place. You need to do it before it's too late!" Janelle replied as Charisma's expression changed.

"Too late? What are you talking about, Janelle?" Charisma asked.

"All I know is God is about to pull back the covers on all the things inside these churches that have been kept under wraps! You need to repent, come clean and own whatever it is you haven't owned up to at this point. If you don't, you're going to wish you had and by then it will be too late!" Janelle said as tears rolled down her face.

"I really don't know what you're talking about Janelle but I don't have anything to hide and I will talk to my kids." Charisma said.

"Okay Charisma, we'll see about that. In the meantime, I'll be having a conversation with them when the time is right. Sis, I love you but if any of your kids tell me about being hurt or abused by one of those people at your church; I will help them report it and get the help they need." Janelle said.

"My kids weren't abused so you won't have to worry about doing that." Charisma told her.

"Yeah, we're going to see about that because I know what I'm feeling in my spirit. You better listen to what I've said, Charisma because your time is winding up." Janelle replied.

The next morning as Charisma laid in her bed sleeping, she heard a text message on her cell phone which was laying on her dresser next to the bed. Charisma initially ignored it until four more text messages came through back to back. She sat up in her bed as she started to yawn and stretch. Charisma grabbed her phone to see who the messages were from and she started to panic when she saw the messages were alerts telling her that her card declined on attempts made to pay her regular bills which Charisma pays with the money she receives from Harold. It never happened before and after checking her bank account and seeing her account in the negative, she knew something was wrong and she didn't know why Harold had suddenly stopped holding up his end of the bargain.

Charisma sent Harold a text message asking him to call her as soon as he was away from his home so they could talk. About ten minutes later, Harold replied with an address to a remote location and told her to meet him there in a half-hour. Charisma quickly showered and got dressed worried about what was going to happen when she talked to Harold. She hadn't worked in years and the money he had been paying her to keep their secret was the reason she was able to live in the house she was in and drive the cars she has. Charisma grabbed her things and quickly headed out to her car but when she opened her front door, an envelope that was lodged into the crease of the door fell to the ground. She quickly picked up, put it in her purse and headed to her car not knowing the level of importance of the letter that was left for her.

She drove as fast as she could to the location and when she arrived, she saw Harold's truck backed into one of the parking spaces with his window down and she parked next to him so they could talk without getting out. Charisma sat and waited patiently as Harold signaled for her to remain quiet while he continued talking to someone on his cell phone. As she waited, she received a text message from one of her half-brothers, Antoine who goes by the nickname *Tone*. He asked her if she received his letter she replied saying that she didn't realize the letter came from him nor had she had a chance to read it. She asked what it was about and why he left it behind instead of just calling her or knocking on the door. Tone took a moment to respond and Charisma quickly glanced back over at Harold who was still on the phone.

Tone responded and said he never received his payment from her and he left the note saying he would tell Chase and her daughters everything he knows if she doesn't pay him by tomorrow. Charisma sighed in frustration as she shook her head and she quickly responded to Tone and begged him not to do that and that she would make sure he got his money as Harold finally ended his call and looked at Charisma.

"So are you done? Why don't I have any money?" Charisma asked in a stern tone.

"Who do you think you're talking to? I'm still your pastor!" Harold replied as Charisma laughed sarcastically.

"Don't throw your title at me right now, where's my money? I have bills to pay so stop playing and put it in my account before I tell your wife who I've really been to you in your church all these years!" Charisma said.

"Charisma, you're not going to say anything because you have as much as to lose as I do and we're both adults now so you would not be able to use the fact that I was way older than you at the time when we started messing around." Harold said.

"Oh yes I can and I will if you don't stop playing with me! Should I call your kids and tell them they have four other siblings their dad never told them about?" Charisma asked.

"Charisma, stop it! You don't need to do anything like that, I'm going to pay you!" Harold said.

"Then if you're paying me, why not just do it instead of having me drive all the way out here?" Charisma asked.

"I had you meet me out here because I need to know the answer to something before I put this money back into your account." Harold said as Charisma sighed and shook her head.

"I don't have all day, I have bills that I need to pay! So what do you want to know?" she asked.

"Who have you been sending $4,000.00 to every month?" Harold asked as Charisma paused a moment before responding.

"I don't know what you're talking about, Harold." Charisma said.

"Charisma, don't play dumb with me! You think I can't see your transaction history? Hello, the account is my name remember? Every month you've been wiring $4,000.00 to someone and you've been doing it for years from what I see. So who are you sending my money to?" Harold asked.

"You wouldn't understand Harold, just let it go. Just know that it's keeping you and I out of harm's way." Charisma said.

"What? Charisma, I'm not scared of anyone! Who are you sending my money to? Tell me now or you won't get anything and if you try to tell everyone about our affair and you having my kids, I'll deny it and falsify reports that will back my statement and have you looking like the town slut! You decide!" Harold said.

"Okay, fine! The money has been going to my brother." Charisma said as Harold's expression changed.

"Your brother? Which one?" he asked.

"Tone..."

"Tone as in your drug dealing brother? Why would you be giving him money when he has money?" Harold asked.

"I still to this day don't know how he got the information but he knows everything. He knows about our affair and he knows that you're my kids' biological father. He told me if I paid him $4,000.00 a month, he would never tell them you were their father so I paid him." Charisma said.

"Charisma, are you serious right now? No one would believe some drug dealer who's been in and out of the system for all these years! He played you!" Harold replied, enraged.

"Call it what you want Harold but my kids love their uncle and if he told them that, they would believe him and it would only be a matter of time before they found a way to confirm it! So I paid him to shut him up and now he's threatening to tell Chase and my girls everything if I don't pay him for this month!" Charisma said as Harold shook his head.

"I should have never got with you, biggest mistake I ever made!" Harold replied.

"Trust me, the feeling is mutual! I can't believe I was foolish enough to think if I had your kids, you would leave your wife and be with me! My role in evangelism was a front for what I really wanted but I'm good now. I don't need a man like you in my life!" Charisma replied.

"Oh Charisma, don't get righteous on me now when you're sitting in the car I bought, wearing the clothes I pay for begging me for the money that pays all of your bills! If you ask me, I am your god!" Harold replied.

"Wow Harold, really? You're really going to call yourself God? Whatever! I'll never call you that but I know you better give me my money and stop playing with me!" Charisma said as Harold sighed and shook his head.

"Check your account Charisma, it's all there now including the extra money for that brother of yours. If I had the manpower, I would take him down myself." Harold said.

"Did you really just sit there and threaten to hurt my brother in front of me?" Charisma asked.

"Yeah I did, so what? You don't care about him! You always said how he was an embarrassment to your family and how you always felt he was the main cause of your parents' stress which led them to both have heart attacks." Harold replied.

"Whatever Harold, I'm done. I got the money so I'm leaving. I really just want out of all of this mess, but I guess I'm about twenty-five years too late." Charisma said.

"Yeah Charisma, you are. It's just part of the price you pay for pleasure. But I'm not worried about you Charisma. You talk a good game but you and I both know you won't ever really open your mouth no matter what happens. You've got just as much to lose as I do if you did." Harold replied with a smirk as Charisma shook her head and drove away in her car.

Charisma didn't want to admit but her pastor was right, she would have just as much to lose if not more if she came clean about the things she's done. Charisma started attending Harold's church when she was 17-years-old after being invited by a girl she went to school with at the time. Charisma's mother never took her and her siblings to church growing up so it was her first time going and it was the first time she met Harold whose father was the pastor of the church at that time. Harold was 32-years-old at the time and he was preparing to take over the church for his father as he got older and started having health problems. Charisma was introduced to Harold and they made an instant connection that Charisma initially felt was innocent. She never had her father in her life and she didn't have the best relationship with her mother so she was enjoying the attention and the love that she was receiving from Harold and she was willing to do anything to keep it. Harold introduced Charisma to his wife, Theresa and their two children and she basically became a part of their family. She joined the church and started attending regularly and she spent a lot of time at their home. Four months later, Charisma and Harold's relationship took an unexpected turn the summer before she started her senior year of high school. Charisma came to church one Sunday and before service started, she walked outside to the back of the building and started crying. She was upset with her mom for spending the money she was supposed to use for senior pictures on cigarettes and alcohol.

Someone spotted Charisma and told Harold where she was and he rushed outback to check on her. He gave her a hug and told her he wanted to be there for her and he told her she could talk to him so she did. Charisma started explaining what happened and Harold told her he would help her and pay for the pictures so she wouldn't have to cancel her appointment. Charisma was excited and appreciative to Harold for wanting to help her but it was what he asked her next that caught Charisma off guard and she didn't know how to respond. Harold asked Charisma what she was willing to do for the money and she asked him what he meant by that. He told her that he's been helping her and was hoping she was willing to do the same for him. He started telling Charisma how beautiful she looked which was something she never heard before. She was a tall, slender brown skin girl whose hair was always pulled back into a ponytail. Charisma's mother was a fair skinned woman who always made Charisma feel that she wasn't pretty because of her skin color so hearing a compliment from a men that she now looked up to was refreshing on many levels and she didn't want that to change by turning him down so Charisma asked Harold what he wanted her to do and that was where it all started.

Harold and Charisma began their affair and in exchange for sex, Harold bought Charisma clothes, he gave her money and he did whatever she asked. No one knew about the affair and everything seemed to be running smoothly until Charisma got sick one day and Harold decided to buy her pregnancy test. Charisma took the test and she found out she was pregnant and she panicked because she knew her mom would kick her out of the house if she found out she was having a baby. Charisma immediately assumed that Harold would pay for her to have an abortion but to her surprise, he didn't do that. He told Charisma that he loved her and that he wanted her to have his child. Charisma was shocked and she couldn't understand why he would want to risk everyone including his wife finding out about their affair so she asked him.

Harold explained at the time that he had a paternity test done on his two children and found out that they weren't his children. He wanted nothing more to do with his wife and they were only going to remain married to maintain their status in the church but Harold convinced Charisma that she was the only woman for him even though he was much older than her. Harold used money from his secret account to buy Charisma the house she lives in now and he bought her a car. Charisma turned eighteen not long after finding out she was pregnant and she dropped out of school after Harold promised to take care of her and their child. Nine months later, Chase was born and they agreed to give him Charisma's last name instead of his so no one would know he was the father. While it is usually common to see people in church turn against a woman who has a child out of wedlock, Harold didn't allow that to happen. Everyone continued to embrace Charisma and offered to help her with her son if she needed it but Charisma knew Harold was taking care of her and their son. Charisma and Harold continued their affair and together and a year later, Charisma gave birth to Ceejai and not long after that she had Channing and Charity.

No one knew that Harold was the father of Charisma's four children except for Theresa. Harold was still bitter about his wife's affair and the fact that she had their children knowing they weren't his so he told her everything and threatened to ruin her life if she ever tried speaking out about it to anyone including Charisma. Theresa was angry and she was hurt but she felt she had no choice but to do what Harold told her because of what she would lose if this truth came out. In addition to their status as prominent pastors in the community, Theresa's parents are well known philanthropists who donate thousands of dollars to multiple organizations nationwide. She couldn't her name or family's name be destroyed by this so she didn't speak. She watched as Charisma continued attending their ministry with the four children she knew were fathered by her husband who is also the pastor of the church. She watched Charisma get ordained and eventually be given the opportunity to take over the Evangelism ministry after attending the church a few years and she couldn't say anything. Theresa knew she was not perfect either, she had an affair with two different men and she knew her husband wasn't the father when she got pregnant but she tried to hide it.

Charisma continued sleeping with Harold up until her thirtieth birthday and that was when her life took another drastic and unexpected turn for the worse. Charisma found someone to keep her children for the night while she went out to a nightclub to celebrate her birthday with her half-sisters; Janelle, Lindsey and Bridgette. While at the club, she had a lot to drink and while she was dancing with an older man she met; he walked her to the back of the club to one of the private rooms. Charisma didn't want her sisters to follow so she texted them and said she was in the bathroom would be back in a moment. Moments after entering the room with this man, he slapped Charisma to the floor and he turned her on her stomach as she started to scream.

The music was loud and no one could hear her as he brutally raped her. He left Charisma on the floor crying and in pain and moments later two women who were walking passed saw her there and called the police and an ambulance. Janelle, Lindsey and Bridgette came looking for her when they went to the bathroom and didn't see her inside. Charisma was taken to the hospital to be treated and because the cameras inside the club weren't working, the detectives only had a description and first name of the man who attacked her. While in the hospital, the doctors performed a minor procedure as a result of the injuries Charisma sustained from the attack. Charisma's life was never the same after that and because of the amount of force her attacker used when he raped her, it left Charisma not being able to engage in sex without being in an extreme amount of pain so she stopped and it ended the affair she was having with her pastor.

Harold was going to kick Charisma and their children out of the house he bought once Charisma was no longer able to have sex with him but he changed his mind when Charisma showed her the documentation she had that would not only expose the fact he was the father of her children but that he started having sex with her when she was still a minor. Harold knew how much he would lose if Charisma said anything so he allowed her to remain in the house and he continued to help take care of their children. Charisma continued in her role at the church and everything was done to keep secrets to maintain their reputation in the church. Charisma's children asked her many times growing up about their father and they wanted to know who he was but she always said that she didn't know anything about their father and she did everything she could to avoid talking about the fact that their pastor was their father. Charisma spent more time at church than she did with her children and she would attempt to make up for disappointing her children on a regular basis by spending money on them and giving them whatever they asked for, not realizing that her children wanted more than nice things. They wanted love, they wanted a genuine relationship with their mother and they wanted their father.

When Charisma finally arrived home, she sat inside of her car for a moment in tears as she thought about her conversation with Harold and everything else that had happened in her life. At her age, she knows she's not innocent and that she hasn't done it all right. But she can't help but feel that her age when her journey began means nothing anymore and it's part of why she never wants to talk about her real feelings to anyone, including her sisters and her brothers. When Janelle left earlier, she sent Charisma a text message saying that she never stopped praying for her to get healed and to receive the help she needed after her attack in the club that night. Charisma knew that Janelle chose to text her instead of bringing it up during their conversation because she knew she wouldn't want to talk about it if she did. Charisma is the oldest of six children and in addition to her three sisters, she has two brothers; William and Antoine who everyone knows as Tone.

Charisma and William have the same father who they only knew was in prison for murder. Her other siblings have different fathers and none of them knew who they were nor did their mom want to talk about it. Charisma's mother died four years ago in Miami after being murdered by a man she owed money to for drugs. Charisma and her siblings have done their best to stick together but there's so much dysfunction between them, they don't have the best relationship with each other all the time. Charisma was a young mother and she hoped to be a better mother to her children than her mother was to her but she found herself repeating some of the same cycles with her own children and she didn't think she could change any of it because she had to cover her pastor and maintain her own reputation as well. Covering her pastor has cost Charisma a lot even with all the money she has. She's 50-years-old and still doesn't know who she is, only what her pastor has identified her to be. Someone who pleasured him and was pressured to do whatever he wanted in order to keep his love and his acceptance of her.

As Charisma finally got out of her car parked in the driveway, she was approached by her neighbor; Marsha as she walked out to her mailbox. Marsha was a sweet older black woman who lived three houses down from where she stayed. Charisma didn't know much about her outside of the fact that she and her husband, Eli were retired pastors who moved to Atlanta from California several years ago. They were both nice people that she would tend to say hello to from time to time.

"Hi Charisma, how are you today?" Marsha asked with a smile as Charisma smiled back slightly.

"I'm doing alright, how are you?" she asked as she closed her mailbox back.

"I'm blessed, God is good!" Marsha replied as Charisma nodded.

"Yes ma'am..."

"Are you just arriving home?" Marsha asked.

"Yes ma'am, I am. I had to take care of some business. Is something wrong?" Charisma asked in a concerned tone after seeing Marsha's facial expression change.

"Well, I don't think so. I just didn't realize you were just getting back. My husband and I went for a walk earlier and as we passed your house, we saw Chase and Ceejai use their key to go inside your house. We didn't see your other thinking it was in the garage and that your kids were coming to visit." Marsha said as Charisma did her best not to panic.

"Wait a minute! Marsha, are you sure it was my two oldest kids you saw?" Charisma asked.

"Yes ma'am, it was them. Eli spoke and they both waived at us! You didn't know they were here?" Marsha asked.

"No ma'am, I didn't know they were here and I wasn't home when they came. Did they drive?" Charisma asked.

"Yes ma'am, they were in a black car but I don't remember all the details. I'm sure the guard knows what kind of car they were in if you want to ask him. Is everything okay?" Marsha asked.

"Yes ma'am, it's fine. Thanks for letting me know but I better get inside. Have a good day." Charisma replied as she quickly turned and rushed inside of her house to see if anything had vandalized or taken.

Everything appeared to be in place so she couldn't understand what made them show up knowing she wasn't home. Charisma immediately called the guard at the front gate and asked for the information on the car they were driving. After he gave it to her, she asked him to remove their names from the guest list and not to allow Chase or Ceejai into their subdivision unless she gave the okay for them to come in. She knew something was up but she couldn't figure out what it was. She changed the password on her security system and she sat down in the quiet room at the back of her home as she began to think on what she was going to do. Moments later she walked into the kitchen to fix herself something to eat and as she turned to the refrigerator she found a note left behind by Chase and Ceejai.

Based on the handwriting, it looked like it was written by Ceejai and the note said that they came for answers and they wanted the truth. It went on to say that if she didn't come clean, she would regret it. Charisma sighed in frustration and quickly text Harold and told him to call when he received her message because it was urgent. Ten minutes later, Harold called her asking her what was wrong and she read the letter and told him that her neighbors saw Chase and Ceejai at her house while they were having their meeting. Harold told Charisma to meet him at the same location they were at earlier in the next hour before ending the call.

****

Chase and Ceejai asked Channing and Charity to come to their apartment once they spent time visiting Janelle and Vincent. Chase and Ceejai were determined to talk to their sisters and tell them what happened and what they found when they went to their mom's house while she wasn't home. Channing and Charity text Chase to let them know they were on the way after they left Janelle and Vincent's home. Chase and Ceejai were nervous about how they would respond because neither of them ever like talking about their mom or the things she's put them through. But Chase and Ceejai were hoping that their mindset may change once they tell them what they found. When Channing and Charity finally arrived at their place, Chase and Ceejai hugged them and the four of them sat at the dining room table and ate some spaghetti and garlic bread that Ceejai had just finished cooking for lunch.

"This spaghetti is great Ceejai, thanks for cooking it!" Channing said as Ceejail smiled a little.
"Thank you Channing, anything for you guys. Are you still eating take out every day at school?" Ceejai asked.
"Well, we were but we met an upperclassman who lives off campus and she cooks all the time! Sometimes we pay her for food she makes instead of buying takeout." Charity replied.
"Wow, she's that good of a cook?" Chase asked.

"Yeah, she is! She told us she's studying Business and Accounting so she can open her own restaurant." Charity replied as Ceejai and Chase nodded.

"Wow, that's pretty cool." Ceejai said.

"Yeah, it is. Do you guys ever think about going back to school? I mean, it's not too late and we know you can do it." Channing said as Chase and Ceejai glanced at each other.

"I'll admit, we do think about it sometimes but we just have a lot going on right now. Our lives are pretty messed up right now guys and we don't see that happening any time soon." Ceejai said.

"Yeah, that's why we're always pushing you guys and doing whatever we have to do as your big brother and big sister to make sure you two get through college and graduate. Don't do what we did." Chase replied as Channing and Charity nodded.

"We appreciate you guys for always looking out for us and we're going to make you and our family proud by finishing. We just want you to pursue your dreams too, it's never too late. Will you at least think about it for us?" Charity asked with a smile.

"You know we can't turn you down so we will and we'll let you know what we decide." Chase said.

"Cool! So what's good? You said you needed to talk to us about something important." Charity said as they continued eating.

"Listen, we know that you both made it clear that you're done trying to address Mom and get her to tell us the truth about stuff with who our dad is and things like that." Chase said.

"Yeah, we are because she doesn't want to be honest and we're not kids anymore! All this stuff about what she doesn't know is some crap! So we don't care to have anything to do with her!" Channing replied.

"Trust us Channing, we get it! That's part of why we don't talk to her either. But what if I told you, we have information that can answer the questions Mom refused to answer. Would you still want to avoid dealing with this?" Chase asked as Channing and Charity glanced at each other.

"What are you saying Chase? Mom finally came clean?" Charity asked.

"No, but we know the truth now and we know why she hasn't talked all these years." Ceejai replied.

"Okay, so what did you guys do to get this information? I mean, did you break into Mom's house or something?" Charity asked.

"Right, I'm pretty sure she changed the locks by now." Channing replied.

"Well, she hadn't and we used our key to get inside." Chase replied.

"You guys went to Mom's house to snoop around? How did you know she wasn't going to be home?" Charity asked.

"We didn't know, we rode through and her Mercedes was gone so we figured she wasn't there. Wherever she was it took a long time because we stayed in the house for like an hour before we left and she still wasn't back." Ceejai said.

"Guys, I don't even know if we care anymore. Mom has been lying for so long and she didn't help us when we needed her most so I'm over it." Charity replied as Channing nudged her and Ceejai glanced at Chase.

"What did you mean by that, Charity?" Chase asked.

"Nothing Chase, I was just saying." Charity said as Channing shook her head.

"If it's nothing then why did Channing nudge you like that? Do you two need to tell us something about Mom?" Ceejai asked in a concerned tone.

"No Ceejai, it was nothing. For real, what did you find?" Channing replied as Chase and Ceejai paused a moment before responding.

"We're not talking any further until you tell us what's really going on! What aren't you telling us about Mom? Did she do something to you when we weren't there?" Ceejai asked as Channing and Charity dropped their heads.

"C'mon you two, you know you can talk to us. Look at us guys, tell us what happened." Chase said as he and Ceejai grabbed their hands.

"You promise not to do anything crazy if we tell you what happened?" Channing asked.

"We promise guys, just talk to us. Please!" Chase replied, anxiously.

"I don't know if you remember this or not but one weekend a few years ago, Aunt Bridgette had that conference to speak at in Miami and we ended up going with them because you and Ceejai were out of town for spring break with your friends." Channing replied.

"Yeah, we remember that weekend. I was a senior in high school that year and Ceejai was a junior." Chase replied.

"Right, Charity and I were both freshman that year. Well, what we never told you was when Mom and Aunt Bridgette got to Miami; they found out about some leadership meet and greet that was taking place before the conference and they wanted to go but didn't want to watch us." Channing replied.

"So what happened?" Ceejai asked.

"They took us to Grandma's house and paid her a thousand dollars to watch us and they told her they would come get us after the service was over. It was odd because we grew up barely seeing Grandma and at first we didn't really care until we got to the house and we saw all these men inside." Channing told them.

"Grandma had a bunch of men inside of her house and Mom still left you there? Did you tell her you didn't want to go?" Chase asked.

"Yeah, we told her we weren't comfortable staying and Mom kept saying it was okay because Grandma would be there to watch us the whole time and she said we wouldn't be left alone at any point." Channing said.

"So what happened after that?" Ceejai asked as Channing glanced at Charity who looked terrified.

"Charity, can you tell them the rest?"
Channing asked as she nodded.

"About a half-hour after Mom and Aunt
Bridgette left for the conference, Grandma said she
needed to go down the street to the store for
something and that she would be right back. We
asked her if we could go too so we wouldn't be alone
with all those guys." Charity said.

"How many guys were in there?" Ceejai asked.

"It was a bunch of them, at least nine or ten. I
think they were having some type of party. Grandma
said we would be okay and she pointed to some guy
and told him to watch out for us until she came back.
Grandma left and that was when it happened."
Charity replied as tears fell from her and Channing's
face.

"It's okay guys, you're doing good. What
happened?" Chase asked.

"I had to use the bathroom so Channing
walked me down the hall and waited outside the door
for me and the next thing I know I hear her
screaming for me. I quickly opened the door and ran
into the hall calling for Channing and I heard a door
nearby slam to one of the guest rooms. I ran up to the
door and tried to go in but it was locked and I could
hear some man telling Channing to shut up and lay
down and I knew based on what the guy was saying
and how she was screaming that he was raping her. I
kept kicking at the door trying to get it up and that
was when another guy ran up to me from behind and
pulled me into the room directly across the hall. I

screamed for Grandma hoping she was back and the guy slapped me and he raped me too." Charity replied as Chase and Ceejai did their best to hold in their tears and not get too upset.

"Guys it's okay, it's okay. So what happened after that? Did Grandma ever come back?" Ceejai asked as she and Chase walked over and sat on each side of Channing and Charity.
"Yeah, she came back after the guys had already left the room. Channing and I were both in pain and we just laid there until she finally came down the hall looking for us. She screamed when she realized what happened and she took me into the room where Channing was and she hugged us and said she was sorry." Charity replied.
"We asked her to call 9-1-1 and she said she couldn't call them because of all the drugs and the guns inside the house. They would arrest her and her dealers and if that happened, more than likely they would kill her in revenge." Channing said.
"Are you serious? Grandma wouldn't call 9-1-1 because she didn't want to get busted with her drugs and weapons? Did she call Mom and Aunt Bridgette?" Ceejai asked.
"Yeah, I remember she kept calling both of their numbers and sending messages for them to call her back. It kept going to voicemail because by this time they were at the conference and since Aunt Bridgette was speaking, she wasn' t going to answer. Grandma locked the door to the room we were in from inside and told us to stay put until Mom and

Aunt Bridgette came back." Charity replied as Chase and Ceejai shook their heads in disbelief.

"I can't believe Grandma did that, I really can't believe it. So what happened after that?" Chase asked.

"Mom and Aunt Bridgette finally showed up to her house around midnight. Channing and I had fallen asleep but we woke up when we heard Mom, Grandma and Aunt Bridgette in the hallway talking about what happened." Charity replied.

"Could you hear what they were saying?" Ceejai asked.

"Not fully because they were arguing. I remember Grandma kept saying that she only left us alone for a few minutes and she didn't think anything would happen. Then I remember Mom and Aunt Bridgette kept freaking out because they were trying to figure out what they were going to do. Next thing we knew, Grandma knocked on the door and told us to come out so we could leave. Mom and Aunt Bridgette grabbed us both and hugged us and we thought that meant she was going to help us and tell the police what happened." Channing said.

"But they didn't do it, did they?" Ceejai asked as the girls shook their heads.

"We got in the backseat and Aunt Bridgette drove because Mom was literally about to have a panic attack and she kept saying I can't believe this is happening again. We had no idea what she meant by that! Do you know why Mom would have said something like that?" Channing asked.

"No, not at all. She said again? Yeah, I don't know. It could be anything with all the secrets our family has but what happened next?" Chase asked.

"Nothing really happened after that. They didn't take us to the hospital, the police or anyone. Mom and Aunt Bridgette kept asking us if we were ready to be strong and push through this. Then they said we couldn't tell anyone what happened or we would all be in trouble and we would be sent to live away with a foster family out of state so never spoke about it." Channing said.

"We're sorry we never told you guys!" Charity said as Chase and Ceejai began to console both of them.

"It's okay guys, you didn't do anything wrong. I am so sorry this happened to you but we're here and no one will hurt you again, we promise!" Ceejai said as she glanced at Chase who nodded in agreement.

"There was one other thing that happened too." Channing said.

"What was that?" Chase asked.

"When it was time for me Charity and I to start applying for colleges, we figured out that Mom and Aunt Bridgette talked to Pastor Harold. They came to meet with us one day and said the church was going to pay for our tuition for all four years." Channing said as Ceejai and Chase reacted to what she said.

"What? Are you serious? They were going to pay your way through college to keep you quiet about what happened at Grandma's house?" Ceejai asked, disgusted.

"Yeah, but we didn't take the money. We kept working our butts off like you taught us and all the money we have came from scholarships we got on our own. We weren't taking their money even though neither one of us had the courage to speak up about what happened." Channing said.

"I'm guessing you don't know who raped you do you?" Ceejai asked.

"No, we don't know and Grandma isn't here anymore to tell us either. Charity and I were eventually able to get tested and thankfully we didn't contract any sexually transmitted diseases from the attack." Channing replied.

"Yeah, we have no idea if those guys used condoms so we just had to be sure." Charity said.

"You did the right thing and we're happy you didn't contract anything either. So in addition to Grandma knowing what happened; Mom, Aunt Bridgette and Pastor Harold also knew?" Ceejai asked.

"Yeah..."

"What about Dr. Theresa, did she know?" Ceejai asked.

"I'm not sure if she knew or not. She wasn't in the meeting we had that day." Charity replied.

"So what were you guys gonna tell us about your visit to Mom's house? I mean I'm sure whatever you found doesn't say anything about what we just told you." Channing said.

"No, we didn't find anything that confirms what you said but we believe you. You know that right?" Chase asked.

"Yeah, we know and we appreciate it after how everything went down." Channing replied.

"I want you guys to look at these papers we made copies off on Mom's copier. She had this stuff stashed in these boxes in some closet space behind the house near the pool." Ceejai said as she and Chase laid everything on the table for Channing and Charity to see.

"Woah! You took all of this without Mom catching you? Wow! What is it?" Charity asked as they started looking through it.

"Most of it are journal entries that Mom started writing when she was seventeen. That was when she first started coming to the church. We made copies of the entire journal, that's why there's so many pages." Chase said.

"We haven't had the chance to read through every page yet but we read enough to find out that Mom lied about who our dad was and we are not not born to different fathers like she said. We have the same father." Ceejai replied as Channing and Charity looked surprised.

"Are you serious? Do we really have the same father? Did this stuff tell you who he was?" Charity asked.

"Yeah, it did. You won't believe this but we've been seeing our father our entire lives and we didn't even know it." Chase said.

"What do you mean by that? Who is he?" Channing asked.

"Pastor Harold Marshall, III is our biological father." Chase said as Channing and Charity paused a moment before responding.

"No way! That can't be! Pastor Harold is our father? How could that even be possible when he's way older than mom?" Channing asked in shock.

"I know you're trying to read everything but we did some reading before you guys got here and basically, Mom met Pastor Harold when she was 17-years-old and he was 32-years-old. They started sleeping together a few months after she came to the church and not long after that, Mom found out she was pregnant with me and she dropped out of school and everything to let Harold take care of her." Chase said.

"Oh my God! He should have gone to jail! He took advantage of a vulnerable teenager? Why would he do that?" Charity asked.

"We don't quite know what started this but with all these papers, it has to be in here somewhere. But yeah, he's our dad and I'm pretty sure this house we grew up in was paid for by him to keep Mom from ever telling anyone that he had an affair with her and fathered all four of her kids." Chase replied.

"This is crazy! So she just had four kids and no one got suspicious, especially with her being so young?" Charity asked.

"Nope, that's how it is in church! These preachers will protect their brand and their reputation at all cost when they're doing dirt. They think they will just carry their sins to the grave and not get exposed but that's about to change in more ways than one!" Ceejai said.

"What do you mean?" Charity asked.

"I mean, we're going to confront Pastor Harold, Mom and Aunt Bridgette about everything and we wanted to see if you wanted in on our plan?" Ceejai asked.

"Wait, did you say Aunt Bridgette? You said you weren't going to bring up the rape!" Channing said.

"Channing, we should let them do it though. I mean, we've been silent long enough don't you think?" Charity asked as Channing sighed and nodded.

"Alright, you can confront them but I can't face any of them right now." Channing said.

"Yeah, neither can I. I'm sorry but it would just be too much." Charity replied.

"That's okay guys, we understand. We know this is a lot, especially after what you just told us." Ceejai said.

"Ceejai, have you ever been raped or molested?" Charity asked.

"No, I haven't." Ceejai said.

"Neither have I." Chase replied as Channing and Charity nodded.

"But don't worry, we're going to make sure they pay for everything." Ceejai said.

"We appreciate you for speaking on our behalf but please be careful and don't do anything too crazy if you can help it." Channing said.

"Yeah, we'll try but they deserve everything we throw at them and if these religious people won't stand up for victims then we will and we will do it at all cost!" Chase replied.

****

Charisma arrives back home after talking to Harold about Chase and Ceejai being inside of her home while she wasn't there. She was going to explain to Harold that she accidentally left the boxes that she kept locked away with all the information proving paternity along with details about the affair sitting inside of her quiet room because she was planning to go through them when she came home and she wasn't expecting her kids to show up. But when she went back to see Harold, she saw his gun sitting on the passenger seat next to him and she didn't want to risk him getting angry and hurting her for being careless so when he asked if she kept the boxes locked up, she lied and told him she did. He told her not to worry and that he would be prepared if Chase or Ceejai try to confront them.

Harold laughed and drove away when Charisma suggested that they gather all four of their children and tell them the truth and make amends. Charisma drove home worried about what would potentially happen if Chase and Ceejai went through the documents and found out the truth on their own. Charisma will eventually see that her suspicions and fears were right and would bring consequences that no one could have predicted. A few minutes after Charisma walked inside of her house, she heard her doorbell ring as she started towards the kitchen. She quickly went to the front window to see who it was and she saw her neighbor, Marsha with her husband and another man that looked familiar to her but she didn't recognize him. She sighed as she reluctantly answered the door.

"Hello again Marsha, hi Eli. What can I do for you?" Charisma asked.

"Hey Charisma, we're sorry to bother you again but I wanted you to meet our grandson. This is Pastor Elijah Williams, he's the senior pastor here in Atlanta at Restoration House Revival Center. Elijah, this is our neighbor Charisma Jordan who we've told you so much about." Marsha said as Elijah and Charisma shook hands.

"It's very nice to finally meet you Evangelist Jordan!" Elijah said, smiling.

"It's nice to meet you too Pastor Williams. How did you know I was an Evangelist? I don't think I ever told Marsha or Eli about that. Oh wow, are you named after your grandfather by chance?" Charisma asked as Elijah laughed a little.

"Yes ma'am, I am but he's always gone by Eli for short. To answer your first question, your sister Janelle and her husband, Vincent are ministers at my church. We talk about you and your kids all the time." Elijah said as Charisma nodded.

"I thought you looked familiar. I think I saw a flier or something with your picture on it. You're the young pastor right?" Charisma asked.

"Well yes, but I'm chosen for this call." Elijah replied.

"Okay, that's fine. I didn't know Marsha and Eli were your grandparents, a small world." Charisma replied.

"Yeah that's true, it is a small world." Elijah told her.

"Charisma, if you had a moment; we wanted to see if you and Elijah could talk a moment alone?" Marsha asked as Charisma's expression changed.

"You want to talk to me?" Charisma asked Elijah in shock.

"Yes ma'am, I do if you will allow me." Elijah replied as Charisma looked at her watch.

"Okay, that's fine. Do you mind sitting out here on the front porch with me?" Charisma asked.

"Sure, that's not a problem." Elijah said as Marsha and Eli said their goodbyes and left them alone to talk.

"Okay Pastor, what's on your mind? Are you here to confirm all the negative things I'm sure my sister tells you about me and my church all the time?" Charisma asked, defensively.

"No ma'am, that's not it at all. Janelle expresses her concerns for you as her sister but she's never spoken negatively about you, your kids or the church you attend." Elijah replied.

"Yeah but you know who my pastor is right?" Charisma asked.

"Yes, I'm aware that you're under Pastor Marshall." Elijah replied.

"Okay and you're like these other pastors who don't like him and are jealous of him right?" Charisma asked.

"I'm not jealous of anyone and I don't dislike anyone either. Does your Pastor and I have a difference of views on the word of God? Yes, big time! But I still have love for him." Elijah said.

"Okay, if you say so. What is this about? Why did you want to talk to me?" Charisma asked.

"Evangelist, you have been on my heart the last month and I've been praying for you and your children." Elijah replied.

"Well, I appreciate you for praying and you can call me Charisma." Charisma replied.

"Okay, Charisma. The Lord spoke to me about you and he led me to come and talk to you today to warn you." Elijah said.

"To warn me? So you must have talked to Janelle." Charisma said as Elijah looked confused.

"No, I haven't talked to her outside of ministry events that are coming up. Did she talk to you or something?" Elijah asked.

"Yeah, she was just here the other day telling me she had a warning from God too about my kids all these things from the past I need to be honest about. Is that what you're about to say?" Charisma asked in a concerned tone.

"Yeah, it's along those lines. Charisma, God didn't give me a bunch of details but He told me that you know what you've been secretive about and you know what you've had to remain silent about concerning your pastor. God says he knows all things and he wants to heal you from the many things you've experienced in your life that you've used being in ministry to cover up the pain. He said your healing will start with your confession and your confession is going to bring a level of restoration to the relationship with you and your children. But you have to do it quickly and not continue to stay silent, even if it means exposing your leader and the church. None of these secrets are worth dying for." Elijah told her as Charisma panicked.

"What? God told you I'm going to die if I don't confess?" she asked, concerned.

"That's not what I'm saying, Charisma. But God did tell me that and death doesn't always mean physical. It could mean mentally or emotionally. But God didn't specifically say what death meant as it pertains to you but don't wait to find out, Charisma. Be honest and come clean! I know I'm not your pastor and you may doubt my ability because of my age but I hope you can trust the Spirit of God that is in me. I am here if you need to talk to me and if you need help walking through the course to your restoration. You just say the word." Elijah replied as Charisma fought back tears.

"I appreciate the support from you Pastor Williams but I'm good, really I am. But I will keep what you said in mind." Charisma told him as Elijah nodded.

"God loves you Charisma, He always has and He's ready to heal you and your children. Things don't have to remain the way they are, I promise." Elijah replied as Charisma agreed with his response.

"Okay Pastor, I will keep that in mind as well. I appreciate you for coming over but I better get going. It was nice to meet you." Charisma said as they shook hands again.

"It was nice to meet you too, Charisma. Here's my card, you call me anytime if you need me." Elijah told her as she nodded and he got ready to leave.

****

Thursday morning, Chase and Ceejai drove Channing and Charity to the airport to catch their flight back to Orlando. While Channing and Charity were happy to finally know the truth about who their biological father was, they wanted no part in helping Chase and Ceejai confront him and their mom because they really wanted to move on with their life and put their painful past behind them. After leaving the airport, they went to Janelle and Vincent's home to see Chase's sons. While there, they met Pastor Williams who had paid Janelle and Vincent a visit as Chase and Ceejai were getting ready to leave. When they arrived back to their apartment, they continued looking through the copies they made of the documents they found at their mom's house the other day as they discussed their plans for confronting their parents.

"I'm glad I listened to you when you told me not to tell Charity and Channing about the guns we bought. They probably would have freaked out like you said." Chase said.

"Yeah, they would have. I mean, I knew they would never snitch on us or anything but Charity and Channing are different from us. They've never been ones to take risks and walk on the wild side like us." Ceejai replied as Chase laughed a little.

"You're right, they were always the ones to play it safe and do everything by the book if they could. But it's okay, that's why I know they're going to finish college and do big things. They won't have to turn out like us." Chase said as Ceejai nodded.

"Yeah, I'm with you on that. I won't lie, I sometimes think about college and trying to go back. But we're out here in these streets getting this money and handling our business." Ceejai said.

"Yeah and nothing can top that! Besides, by the time we finish handling our parents; we won't be able to worry about school." Chase said as he continued looking through the documents with Ceejai.

"That is true! They're going to pay for what they've done and their little organization won't be able to save them this time!" Ceejai said, glancing at her gun sitting on the table near them.

"I never thought I would have to say this but you know we have to add Aunt Bridgette to our list right? I mean, she didn't do anything to help our sisters when they got raped and that is actually pretty shocking to know. I mean, Aunt Bridgette always looked out for us but just like our mom and our deadbeat father; that church of theirs is more important than us!" Chase replied in a stern tone as he took another sip of his beer.

"Yeah, it's pretty messed up. But you're right, we're adding Aunt Bridgette to the list too. Channing and Charity may not want to get involved but we still want to fight for them." Ceejai said as Chase paused and stared at one of the documents he picked up. "Bro, you good? What happened?"

"Oh my God! Really Uncle Tone, really?" Chase asked, enraged as he slammed the papers on the table and Ceejai walked over to see what was making him so upset.

"What is it Chase? What did you find?" Ceejai asked.

"Look at these bank statements from Mom's account. You see down here where it has the amounts and the names of people she transferred money to?" Chase asked as Ceejai looked through the paperwork.

"Mom has been sending four grand to Uncle Tone every month for the last several years from what I can see. But why? Uncle Tone has money!" Ceejai replied, confused.

"Ceejai, look at the dates on this statement. Tell me what you see!" Chase replied as he walked into the kitchen to get another beer.

"This is dated a year after Charity was born! Chase, this makes no sense! Mom was always trying to keep us away from Uncle Tone, telling us how he was in the streets and up to no good but she sent him $4,000.00 a month? Why?" Ceejai asked.

"Think about it Ceejai, four thousand of the hush money that Pastor Marshall had been giving our mom to stay quiet about their affair and the four of us being his kids! Think about it!" Chase said as Ceejai paused and thought for a moment.

"Oh my God, Chase he was in on it too!" Ceejai said.

"There you go! Uncle Tone knew the whole time that Pastor Marshall was our father and he obviously knew about the affair and he said nothing to us, knowing we wanted to know who our dad was! He let Mom pay him to keep quiet but was the main one saying how he can't stand hypocrites in the church! He can't stand them but didn't mind taking money he didn't even need and for what?" Chase asked, enraged as he kicked one of the chairs over and began pacing the floor. Ceejai shook her head in disbelief.

"Chase, I'm mad too but I hope you're not planning to go after him for this. He has way more manpower than we do and if we attack, we'll die!" Ceejai replied.

"I know that, we're not going to ambush him the same way but we are going to get revenge and he's a dead man walking. I just need to know you're in this with me!" Chase said.

"As long as we don't get hurt or get caught, I'm in. Let's start coming up with our plan on how we're going to get this done." Ceejai replied as Chase nodded and kissed Ceejai on her forehead.

Later that night, Chase and Ceejai left their apartment to attend a party at one of their friend's houses. When they arrived, there were several people gathered inside and outside of the house and cars were parked everywhere. As Chase and Ceejai got out of their truck and started up the sidewalk, they saw Tone getting back into his truck after making a deal with one of the guys at the party. Chase walked back to his truck to grab a large knife he had under the seat after he and Ceejai agreed to make their move on Tone while he was still here so they wouldn't have to drive to his house tomorrow. As the people outside started to walk around back, Chase and Ceejai put their hoods on and decided to approach Tone's truck from behind so he wouldn't see them approaching. As they waited in a set of bushes outside of his parked truck, they could hear Tone on the phone with someone and could see him holding his gun in his right hand. Chase and Ceejai decided to speak and have a casual conversation with him first as Ceejai got in the front seat while Chase got in the back.
Moments later it happened, Chase abruptly grabbed his uncle's head and slit his throat with the knife he was carrying as Ceejai sat looking out and making sure no one was walking nearby. Chase quickly wiped the blood off the knife with a towel he found on the back seat as he and Ceejai quickly got out of the truck and ran back through the wooded area that would lead them to where their truck was

parked on the other end of the street without being seen by anyone. After Chase placed the knife back under his seat, he and Ceejai headed back to the party to avoid any suspicion from anyone in the event that Tone's body was found. Tone came to the party alone but he was there to sell drugs so Chase and Ceejai knew it would only be a matter of time before someone else at the party would start to look for him. As tough as Chase and Ceejai are, this was the first time they actually killed someone. They've robbed people before and held guns on people to scare them but they never thought the day would come where they would actually commit murder and it shocked them even more that their first murder was to a family member they always looked up to and thought they could trust.

An hour later, Chase and Ceejai were going to leave and head home for the night until one of their friends ran up to them in a panic and said the police were outside getting ready to approach Tone's truck which was parked on the street still running with the doors locked and the windows up. A passerby made the call requesting an officer make sure whoever was inside the truck was okay not knowing the person was already dead. Chase and Ceejai's friend turned down the music and told everyone to hide whatever drugs or weapons they had until the police left because he figured they would come knocking on their door since Tone's truck was parked near the house. Chase and Ceejai looked out to see what the officer was doing as he talked on his radio and gave information to the dispatcher. Another officer arrived to assist and that was when the officer broke the driver side window. Chase and Ceejai knew they found Tone's lifeless body inside the truck when the two officers quickly stepped back and started calling for backup. As more officers started to arrive, everyone inside the house walked outside to see what was going on as Chase and Ceejai stood on the steps waiting to see what was going to happen next. Moments later, four detectives walked over to where everyone was standing to announce that Tone was found dead inside of his truck with his throat slashed. They went on to say that based on his body temperature, it appeared that this murder had just happened an hour or so ago.

Everyone reacted to the news in shock as the detectives did what they could to calm everyone down as they began to ask questions. No one wanted to talk and everyone claimed that they knew nothing about what happened. Others said they didn't know who Tone was or that he was at the party while a few more people told the detectives that they should talk to Chase and Ceejai because Tone was their uncle. Chase looked at Ceejai and told her to stay calm and follow his lead as they talked to the detectives so they could keep their stories straight. One of the detectives asked Chase and Ceejai if they would be willing to meet them at headquarters to answer some questions after it was made clear that they weren't suspects and they agreed to meet them there. Chase and Ceejai quickly walked out to their truck and sat inside for a moment before leaving the location.

"Chase, did you want to call Aunt Janelle and the rest of our family now or later?" Ceejai asked as Chase sighed and thought for a moment.

"No, I'm pretty sure the news crew will be out here in a minute to get a story so they can find out that way. Or if not, I'm sure Uncle Tone had our mom or one of our other aunts and uncles listed as emergency contact so let the police tell them. We need to focus on making sure our stories are straight when we get downtown because we're probably going to be questioned separately." Chase replied as Ceejai nodded.

"I know..."

"Are you okay? I know that was a lot." Chase said as he grabbed her hand.

"Yeah, I'm okay. I never killed anyone before." Ceejai replied.

"I know. I never did it before either and I know Uncle Tone wasn't initially on our hit list but we were gonna be taking some lives to get revenge remember?" Chase asked as Ceejai nodded.

"Yeah, I know. So what are we telling the police?" Ceejai asked as Chase cranked up his truck and drove away from the location.

"Since neither of us contacted Uncle Tone by phone prior to arriving at this party, we're going to tell the police that we didn't know he was there until they came up to tell us the news. There were a lot of cars out there and we didn't realize his truck was parked on the street." Chase said.

"Okay, I'll make sure I say that." Ceejai replied.

"Yeah, if we tell them we knew he was there they're going to ask why and we can't out our friends like that. I hope they were able to hide those drugs and guns like they said." Chase replied.

"I mean, the police can't enter without a warrant right?" Ceejai asked.

"I think so, I never know how that stuff works at times. But let's just go do this interview and move on with the rest of our plans. If we keep being discreet like we did back there, nothing will stop us when we go after Mom, Pastor Marshall and Aunt Bridgette." Chase replied as Ceejai nodded in agreement.

****

It's been a month since the murder and funeral of Charisma's youngest brother, 42-year-old Antoine *"Tone"* Jordan, Sr. Police have not been able to link anyone to his murder and are assuming that it was possibly someone he knew from his dealings in the streets who wanted revenge or a drug deal that turned deadly. The call logs on his phone showed that the last call he made before his murder was to his three children who live with their mother in Miami. Chase and Ceejai had chosen to wait until the police completed their investigation with their uncle before executing their plan to confront Charisma, Harold and Bridgette. Charisma came home after meeting with Janelle, Bridgette and the rest of their siblings about Tone's passing and what they were hoping they could do to make sure his case doesn't turn cold as a result of him being a well-known drug dealer in the city. As Charisma got out of her car and walked down to her mailbox, she saw Marsha walking towards her with what appeared to be a letter that she had in her hand.

"Hello Charisma, how are you?" Marsha asked.

"I'm doing okay, still grieving my brother. How are you?" Charisma asked.

"I'm good. Just know that we have been praying for all of you guys, I know this hasn't been easy to deal with and we're here if you need us." Marsha replied as Charisma nodded and smiled a little.

"Yes ma'am, we appreciate that. Thank you. You, Eli, Pastor Williams and his church have been more than generous and nice to us during this time. I mean, I know Janelle goes to his church but you've been there for all of us which means something." Charisma replied.

"Of course, that is what the Body of Christ is supposed to do for each other! Listen Charisma, I won't hold you long but Elijah came by to see us earlier and he wrote this letter to you and asked if I could give it to you when he saw you weren't home." Marsha said, handing the letter to Charisma as her expression changed.

"Oh wow, Pastor Williams wrote this to me?" she asked in shock.

"Yes ma'am, he did. I didn't read it so I don't know what it says but he said to tell you that it was

important that you read it." Marsha replied as
Charisma nodded.

"Okay, I'll go inside and read it now then.
Thank you, Marsha. Have a good day." Charisma said
as she and Marsha hugged each other before she
walked towards her house.

Charisma decided to walk around back to the
patio area near the pool as she opened the envelope
and began to read the letter that Pastor Williams left
for her. As she sat down, she couldn't help but
wonder what it was he had to say to her again. The
letter read...

Dear Charisma,
I want to start off by offering my sincerest condolences
again to you and your family for the passing of your
brother, Antoine. I know losing a loved one is never
easy to deal with and we are definitely praying and
here to support your family during this time.
Charisma, I know it has been a while since you and I
had a chance to speak and I'm not sure if you took
anything I said before to heart but I hope that you have.
What I shared with you then is more imperative to
your life now than it was when I first felt the Holy
Spirit lead me to share it with you. As I wrote this
letter to you, I prayed and allowed God to give me the
words to speak as He did before because I know that
there's a lot about your life that many (including
myself) know nothing about. But your Heavenly Father
is well aware and as I told you before He desires to heal

those places in your soul and make you whole again. He desires for your son and your three daughters to be healed and made whole again as well. I had the pleasure of meeting Chase, Charisma (Ceejai), Channing and Charity and they are amazing. Your grandsons are amazing as well and I can see the purpose of God that is in each of their lives. I know that you desire to have the broken relationship with them restored. God wants to make that happen but it's going to take your confession for this healing journey to really start. The confession may be hard to say and the truth will be hard to own but it must be done and it's imperative that you do it even if it means exposing your own leader and ministry in the process. Your soul and the souls of others are at steak if you don't heed the warning God is using me to give you in this letter. God told me that there is a truth that will be exposed in the worst way if you don't take a stand and speak up. So please, hear the word of the Lord and don't let fear of what your pastor or others will say stop you from obeying what God is saying and has been saying to you. I love you with the love of the Lord and I am praying for you always.

Sincerely,
Pastor Elijah Williams

Charisma began to cry hysterically after reading Pastor Williams' letter because deep down, she knew that everything he said was right. But even with the warnings that Charisma had been receiving from Pastor Williams, she didn't feel she could risk the reputation of her church and her pastor by telling the truth. She couldn't see that her silence and refusal to come clean was no longer helping keep her many secrets in the dark but it was slowly but surely coming to the light in a way that no one could anticipate and the window for her to be honest and help her children was closing in quickly. When Charisma woke up for church Sunday morning, she got dressed as normal not knowing that today would be a day of reckoning for her in more ways than one. She was getting ready to see the price she chose to pay all of these years at the expense of her own children just to cover her pastor and maintain a status inside the church.

Service didn't begin until noon but Harold called a leadership and requested that everyone meet him at the church by ten but he asked her and Bridgette to come to his office at nine so they could discuss another matter. Charisma didn't ask at the time but she was pretty certain they were going to discuss a plan for confronting Chase and Ceejai to find out what information they gathered the day they came to Charisma's home while she wasn't there. When Charisma arrived at the church, Chase and Ceejai were parked in their truck in a hidden area near the church watching as she and Bridgette got out of their cars and walked inside the church to meet with Harold before the rest of the leaders arrived. Chase and Ceejai quickly put on their gloves as they went over their plan again before going inside. They were both dressed in black suits as part of their disguise and moments later, they got out of the truck and started across the street towards the back door of the church. After walking inside and seeing that no one was in the hall, Chase and Ceejai pulled out their guns and started to quietly walk towards the other end of the sanctuary where Harold's office was located. Moments later they arrived at his office door and could hear Charisma, Harold and Bridgette inside having a conversation as Ceejai waited for Chase to give her the signal for when they would go in. Chase nodded and they both entered Harold's office with their guns drawn as he, Charisma and Bridgette quickly put their hands up and stood against the wall as Ceejai closed and locked the door behind them.

"Don't scream and don't even think about calling the police or we will shoot you right where you stand!" Chase said as he and Ceejai kept their guns drawn on them.

"Kids, what are you doing? We can talk about this!" Charisma said, afraid of what they might do.

"Oh so now you want to talk, Mom? What if I told you we're done talking and we're tired of the lies you've been telling us all of our lives!" Chase said.

"Son, calm down! You and Ceejai don't have to do this!" Harold pleased as Chase gave a smirk.

"Wow, you called me son! That's very fatherly of you now isn't it, DAD!" Chase said as Bridgette's expression changed and she glanced at Harold and Charisma who were both shaking their heads.

"Yeah Aunt Bridgette, we don't have different fathers like Mom led you to believe. You both have been in church with our dad this entire time!" Ceejai replied.

"No way! Charisma, they're lying right? Please tell me this isn't true! You and our pastor?" Bridgette asked, disgusted.

"Sis, you don't understand. A lot of stuff happened that you don't know about." Charisma said.

"Charisma, keep your mouth shut! Bridgette, are you really going to believe them over us?" Harold asked.

"SHUT-UP! You sat up here and dressed up lies behind your big church, your money and all of your accolades and you did it at our expense! You didn't care enough about your own kids to tell the truth so you've lied all these years thinking you would never get exposed but that is changing today!" Chase said.

"I still can't believe what I'm hearing right now!" Bridgette replied.

"That's fine Aunt Bridgette because we have your proof right here!" Ceejai replied tossing the documents they took from Charisma's house to Bridgette who was sitting between Charisma and Harold.

"You took advantage of our mom when she was 17-years-old and you were in your thirties and you cheated on your wife with her! Then she got pregnant with me and for some strange reason, you decided to help her cover up the fact that she was pregnant with your child by putting her up in that nice house and paying for everything instead of just having an abortion! Then to add insult to injury, you have three more children with her, all behind your wife's back!" Chase said.

"At least we think it was behind her back! I mean, I don't know what woman would stay in marriage with a man who slept with a teenage girl and had children with her. Mom, you drug us to this church week after week knowing Harold was our father and you never told us! You told us you didn't know who our dad was and that you had multiple partners and it was a lie! You told us Grandma left you money in her insurance policy after she died and that's why we were able to afford the house and those cars but that was a lie! Harold paid you all this money and gave you the house and the cars to keep you quiet about us!" Ceejai said as Bridgette shook her head in disbelief.

"I can't believe you two did this! Wow!" Bridgette said.

"Oh Aunt Bridgette, you may not have had anything to do with that situation but you're not innocent either and you're hanging on this same limb with your sister and your beloved pastor!" Chase said as Bridgette's expression changed.

"What are you talking about? I didn't know Harold was your father! Charisma lied to me too!" Bridgette said.

"It's not about this Aunt Bridgette! See, Channing and Charity told us what happened in Miami that weekend you had to preach and you wanted to impress your pastor friends so you left our sisters with Grandma and all those men she was running with in the streets at the time!" Chase said.

"Oh my God! Chase, let us explain! Please, it's not what you and Ceejai may be thinking! A lot happened that you don't know about." Bridgette replied.

"Oh no Aunt Bridgette, you never tried explaining before so we're not trying to hear it! Channing and Charity told us everything when they came to visit a couple of months back. They were both raped by guys at Grandma's house while she was at the store and when you and Mom came to pick them up, you were more focused on keeping them silent so you could cover your pastor and the church than you were on making sure they got the help they needed!" Chase replied as Bridgette started to cry.

"You can spare us those tears, all of you! They're fake and it's not for us but it's for yourselves. You don't feel bad about any of this and had we not found out the truth on our own, you would have tried to carry this to the grave!" Ceejai replied.

"Yeah and now you get to go to the grave knowing that all of your secrets will be exposed to the world and people are going to see you for the crooked church you really are!" Chase said.

"You're not going to kill us are you? I'm your mother, we're your family!" Charisma said in fear.

"No, a mother doesn't lie to her kids. A mother doesn't leave her daughters in an unsafe environment to get raped and then tell them to stay quiet about it! So yeah, you're not leaving here alive!" Chase said as Ceejai gave a smirk.

"So tell us Mama, was all of this worth dying over? Why didn't you just come clean? We would have been mad but we wouldn't be holding guns on you right now had you just told the truth but you didn't do it and you tried paying off our uncle to keep your little secret too but that didn't work either as you can see!" Ceejai said as the three of them reacted to what Ceejai said.

"I knew it! You killed your uncle when you saw my bank statements didn't you? You saw the money I was sending him and you put two and two together!" Charisma said as she cried more.

"What? Is this what this is about? You told me you had your papers locked up in your house, Charisma! That's where they got these documents from?" Harold asked in shock.

"I'm sorry Harold, I am so sorry. It wasn't supposed to happen like that but I can't believe you murdered your uncle and let the police think it was some drug deal gone bad! You're wrong!" Charisma said, enraged.

"No, you guys are wrong! We're just getting revenge and getting street justice for what happened to Channing and Charity even though they didn't want to confront you because they're trying to move on. But we're getting revenge for them!" Chase said.

"So they don't know you're doing this?" Charisma asked.

"No they don't know we took it this far but they will soon find out!" Chase replied.

"Guys, please don't do this! Think about your cousins and them being without their mother if you kill me!" Bridgette said as Chase and Ceejai started laughing.

"Aunt Bridgette, who do you think gave us the tip about you guys getting to church early? Yeah, we talked to our cousins (*your daughters*) and they're not too happy with you either because they were molested by your beloved pastor here and you told them they were lying and you told them not to bring it up again! Remember that?" Ceejai asked as Charisma glanced at them.

"You touched her daughters? Are you serious right now?" Charisma asked in shock.

"Yeah I think Harold is a little speechless right now because he didn't know his little secrets would come out like this. All I'll say is I hope your silence was worth dying for because we're here to get vengeance and even if it's from the grave, we're here to make you pay!" Chase said as he drew his gun again.

"Prepare to meet your maker!" Ceejai replied.

THE AFTERMATH
Four Months Later

It's been four months since Chase Jordan, Sr. & Charisma *"Ceejai"* Jordan were arrested and charged for the brutal murders of their uncle, Antoine *"Tone"* Jordan, Sr., their aunt, Prophetess Bridgette Jordan and their parents, Pastor Harold Marshall & Charisma Jordan. Chase and Ceejai had no remorse for what they did and were forthcoming to the police about everything that happened when they arrived at the church to respond to a report from an anonymous caller about multiple gunshots that were heard from the church. Even though Chase and Ceejai weren't requesting to be represented by attorneys because they didn't care what happened to them, Janelle's husband, Vincent called his brother-n-law who is one of the best defense attorneys in the state and paid him to represent Chase and Ceejai when they stood before the judge at trial.

With his help, they didn't receive the death penalty and were only sentenced to ten years of probation and would not have to serve any time in prison for the murders they committed. Their victory was short lived after walking out of the courthouse with their lawyer and several reporters when the unthinkable happened and shots were fired. After everyone fell to the ground, Janelle looked over and screamed when she saw the attorney and officers starting to surround Chase and Ceejai who were both lying on the ground bleeding severely after being shot in the chest by their cousin, Antoine who was Tone's son. He fell to his knees in tears as the officers quickly took the gun and arrested him.

The ambulance rushed Chase and Ceejai to the hospital but they died on the way after succumbing to their injuries losing too much blood. The story made headlines all over the world as one local reporter who decided to title her story *"To Die Four!"* where she wrote about the secrets that started with an affair between a pastor and one of his members that resulted in four children being born and kept a secret in order to maintain the reputation of the pastor and the ministry. The lies and the silence of one mother who was willing to cover her pastor at the expense of her own children created chaos that would ultimately result in the exposure of this pastor through murder. As Janelle and her husband, VIncent continue to raise Charisma's grandsons and help Channing and Charity get the help they need as they grieve and process what has taken place; it is her prayer that this story will not just be a topic of discussion for the next gossip column.

Janelle is praying this story will bring awareness to the church and cause the hearts of people to be convicted and will confess what they have done when they have sinned against God through the offense and abuse of others. No sin, big or small is worth hiding from God and those involved. There is power in confession and warning will always come before destruction! But it is up to those that have received the warning to respond and adhere to what God is saying before it is too late and souls are lost.